W9-BAP-194

Weekly Reader Children's Book Club presents

MR. YOWDER AND THE STEAMBOAT

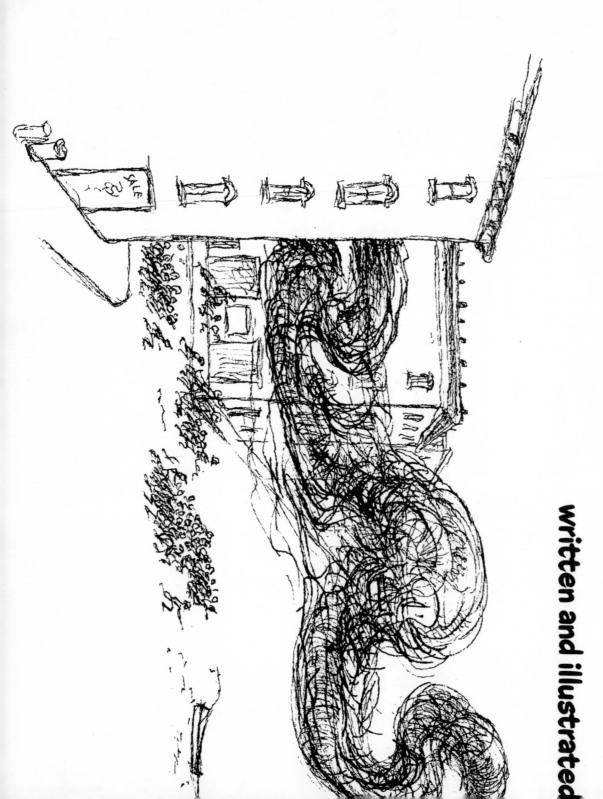

MR. YOWDER AND THE

written and illustrated

STEAMBOAT

by GLEN ROUNDS

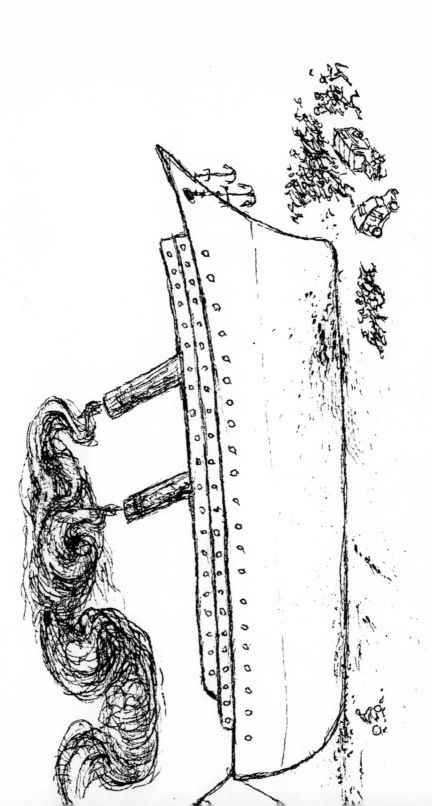

Holiday House · New York

FOR

KATE

Copyright © 1977 by Glen Rounds.
All rights reserved.
Printed in the United States of America.

Library of Congress Cataloging in Publication Data

Rounds, Glen, 1906-

Mr. Yowder and the steamboat.

SUMMARY: A friendly card game becomes a disaster
for a steamboat captain and his pilot.

[1. Boats and boating—Fiction. 2. Humorous
stories] I. Title.

PZ7.R761Mk [Fic] 76-43089

ISBN 0-8234-0294-0

Weekly Reader Children's Book Club Edition

Mr. Xenon Zebulon Yowder always spoke of himself as being THE WORLD'S BESTEST AND FASTEST SIGN PAINTER, and perhaps he was.

His usual home range was west of Kansas City, Missouri, south to Texas, north to Montana and the Dakotas, and west as far as his fancy might take him.

But at the time I speak of, he was wintering in New York City, New York. That is about as far east as one can get, but how it came about he never did say. It seems, however, that he'd rented him a nice room in a boarding house not far from one of the two rivers that run on either side of that town.

The way Mr. Yowder told it later, his adventure with the steamboat started one morning when he happened to ask his landlady, a widow woman named

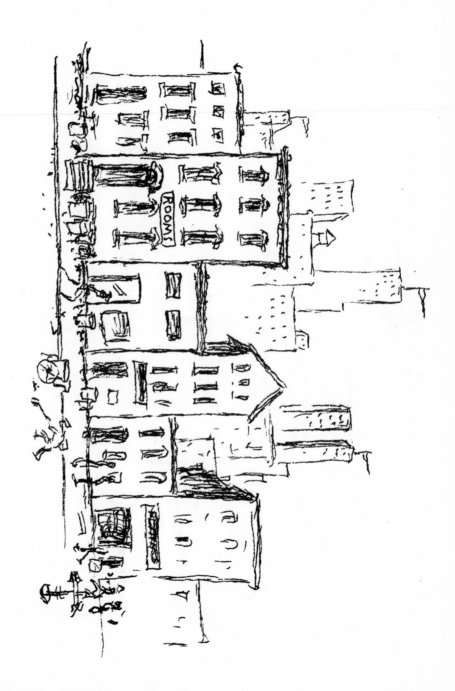

O'Leary, if there were any fish down there in the river. She said the fishing was known to be very good at that time of year, and should Mr. Yowder take a notion to go catch a mess, she'd cook them up for his supper.

Mr. Yowder had always liked to fish, so he borrowed a fish pole the landlady had stored in the basement and hurried down to the river right after breakfast.

But he found all the good places along the bank were already taken, so he decided to rent him a rowboat, figuring that there should be plenty of good fishing holes further out in the river.

There are not many places in a town like New York City, New York, where a man can dig fishing worms, so to save time, he bought some from the man that rented him the boat.

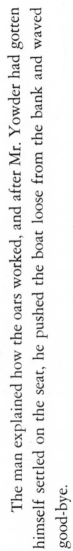

The man explained how the oars worked, and after Mr. Yowder had gotten himself settled on the seat, he pushed the boat loose from the bank and waved good-bye.

At first Mr. Yowder had some trouble trying to pull on the oars while looking back over his shoulder to see where he was going. But soon he got the hang of it and rowed briskly out into the river.

However, finding a quiet fishing hole turned out to be no easy matter, for that river was crowded with boats. There were boats of all sizes, he said—small, middle-sized and so big you'd not believe it. And they were going in all directions. There were boats going upstream, and there were boats going downstream. There were boats going back and forth across the river, and still others that didn't seem to be going anywhere in particular—just messing around.

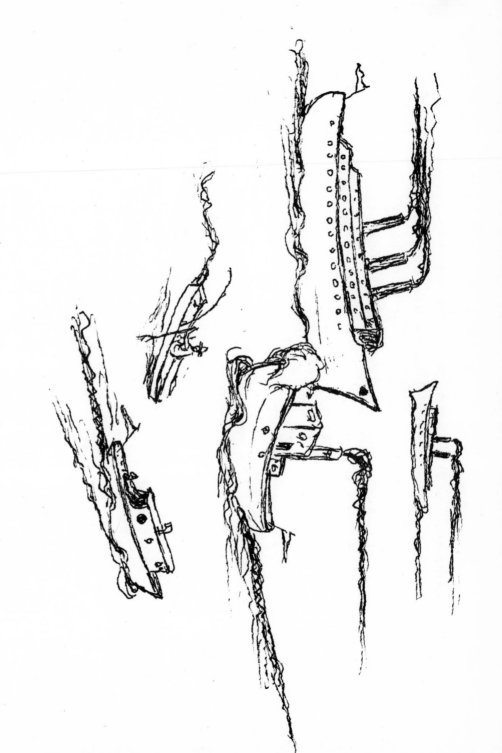

Mr. Yowder would no sooner find himself what looked like a good place to fish and start baiting his hook, than he'd hear the roar of a whistle and look up to find himself directly in the path of a boat bigger than Bearpaw Smith's store back home in Lonetree County. He spent most of his time rowing frantically, first in one direction and then the other, to keep from being run over.

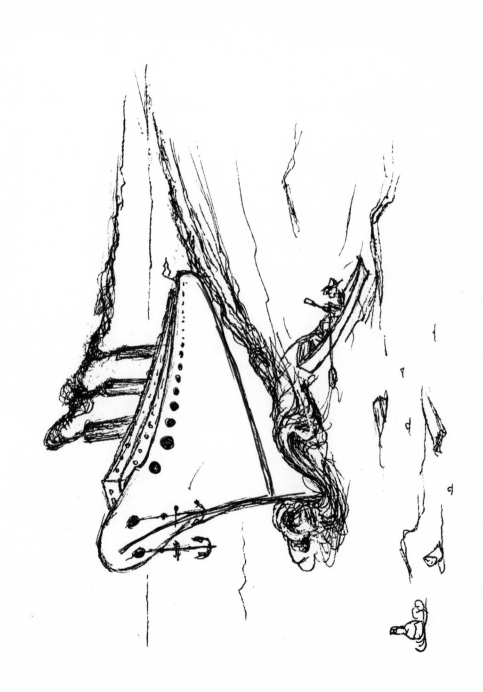

For a while he was so busy trying to keep out of the way of all those boats, that he didn't notice the brisk current carrying him towards the mouth of the river. But when he did have time to stop and look around, he found he was a mile or two below town and well out onto the ocean—which he'd never seen before. At last he'd gotten away from the boats; there wasn't one in sight anywhere.

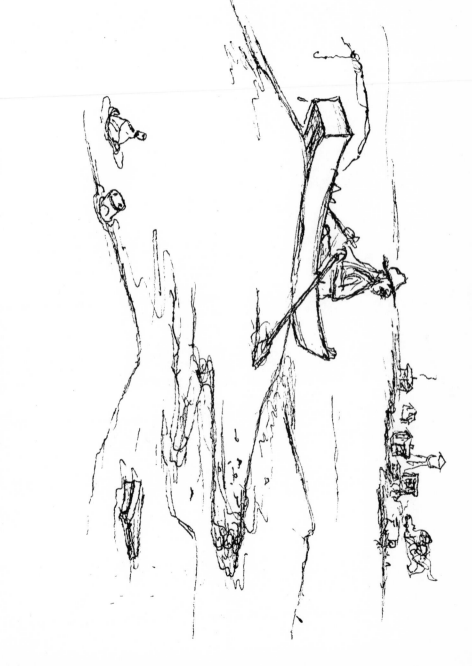

But even so, his troubles were not over—he quickly discovered that the ocean is by no means flat like one expects water to be. Instead, it was all hills—hills of water in any direction he looked. And worst of all, the hills did not stay still. He'd no sooner row up to the top of one and stop to look around, than the thing would slither out from under his boat and leave him in a swale again!

He rowed this way and that way, up one hill and down another, looking for a level place where he could stop and fish. But there were no level places—nothing but water going uphill and downhill. And then, for some reason, his stomach began to feel a little queasy, so he decided he'd best turn around and go back.

But when he looked around, he discovered he was out of sight of land. Of course there were no signposts out there, nor any landmarks of any kind, so he had no idea how he was going to find the way back to town.

He was lost.

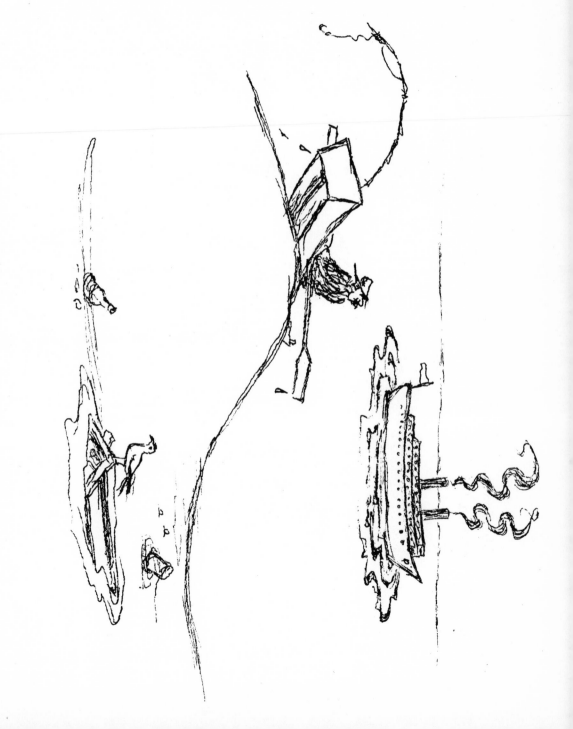

But about that time, he saw a big steamboat standing still in the water off to his left a half a mile away. So he decided to row over and ask them the way to town.

When Mr. Yowder got up close to the steamboat, he couldn't see anybody on it. But he hollered and banged on the side with an oar, and pretty soon a man wearing a cap with a lot of gold embroidery on it leaned over the rail and asked him what he wanted.

Mr. Yowder explained that he was lost, and could the man direct him to New York City, New York.

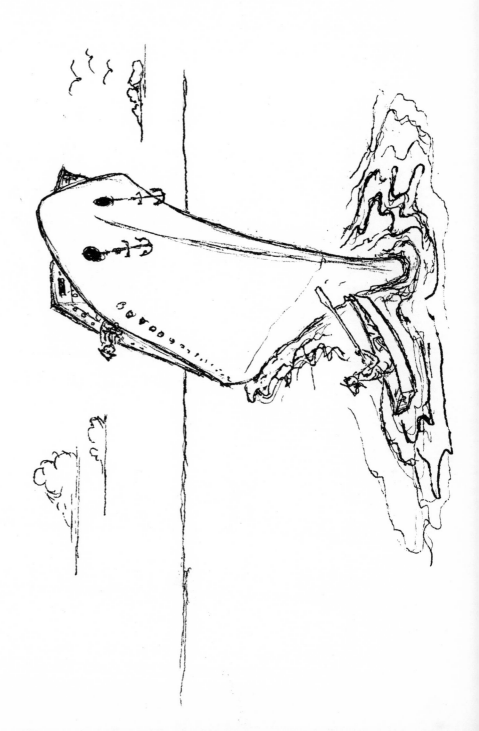

The fellow explained that he was Captain of the steamboat and was going that way himself, just as soon as his hired man fixed the engine trouble they were having at the moment. He went on to say that if Mr. Yowder wasn't in a big hurry, he was welcome to tie his boat on behind and ride back to town with him. So Mr. Yowder tied his boat to a long rope hanging down at the back of the steamboat, and the Captain let down a ladder so he could climb up on top.

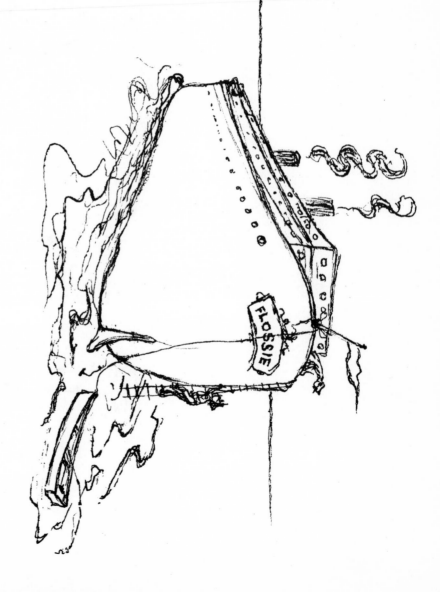

Mr. Yowder remarked that he was right handy with machinery himself, so he and the Captain went downstairs to where they kept the engine, to see if they could help the hired man.

The three of them, working together, soon found the trouble and got the thing to running. It still missed on one cylinder, but the Captain said it should get them into New York City all right. So leaving the hired man to run the engine, the Captain and Mr. Yowder went back upstairs to what the Captain called the Bridge. That was the place he drove the steamboat from.

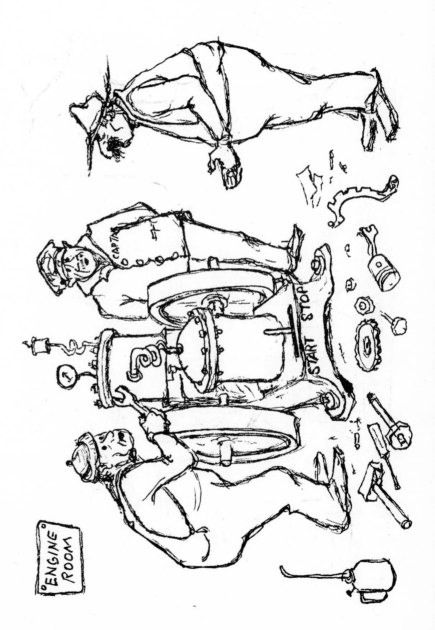

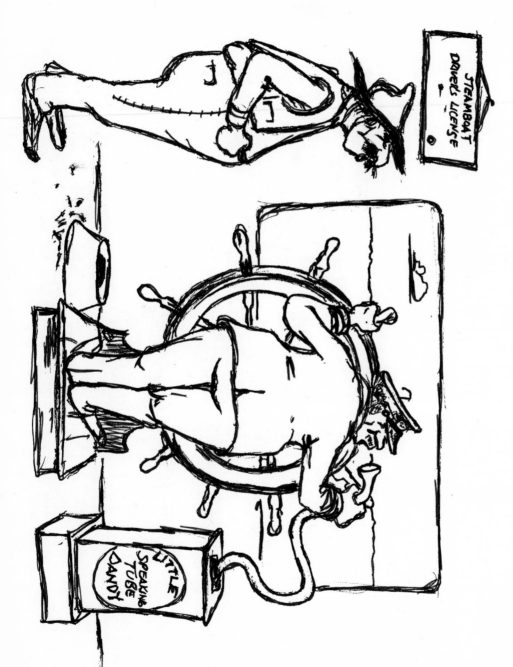

It was a room with big windows, high up in the front of the boat. The Captain walked up to a steering wheel as high as he was, looked at a big compass to see which way the steamboat was pointing, then hollered down a speaking tube and told the hired man he was ready to start.

He turned the steering wheel this way and that for a while, until he had the steamboat going the way he wanted, but after that there wasn't much to do. So he brushed some maps and newspapers off a little table, got out some cards and asked Mr. Yowder if he'd like to play a few games just to pass the time. Mr. Yowder explained that he wasn't much of a card player, but if they just played for matches, it was all right with him.

That steamboat was so big, it sort of cut through the hills of water instead of going up and down like Mr. Yowder's rowboat had done, and his stomach began to feel better.

Sometimes, when it was Mr. Yowder's deal, the Captain would get up to speak down the speaking tube to the hired man about the engine, or to blow the whistle at some boat going by. But mostly they just played cards.

At first they played for matches, but after a while the Captain suggested playing for money—nickels and dimes, perhaps—just to make the game more interesting.

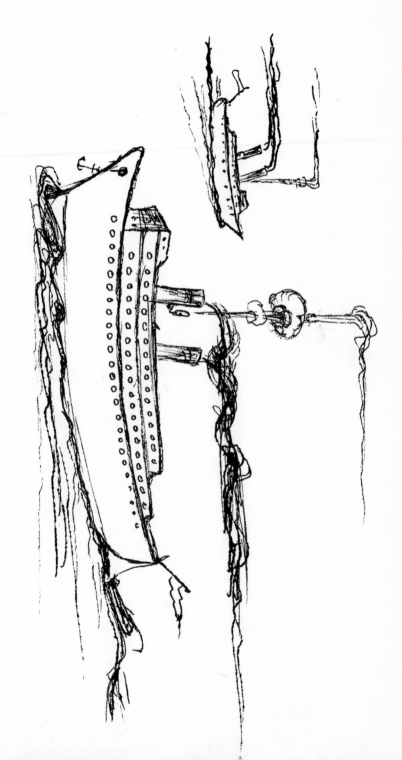

It turned out that the Captain wasn't a very good card player, and before long Mr. Yowder had won all the change he had on him—a dollar and seventy-six cents, his penknife and a gold-trimmed goose quill toothpick he was very proud of.

Then they played for the Captain's official gold-embroidered captain's cap, and Mr. Yowder won again.

When Mr. Yowder took off his old Stetson and saw himself in the mirror wearing that fancy cap, he was right pleased with the change in his appearance.

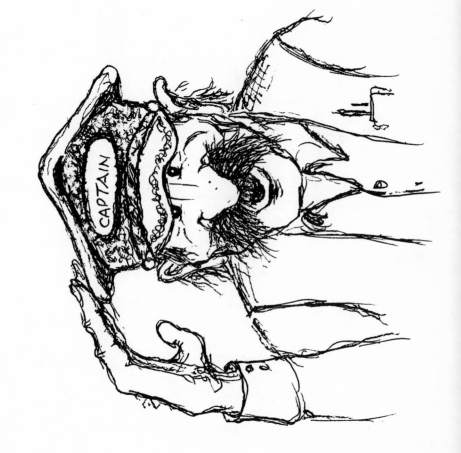

The Captain still did not want to stop playing, so next they played for his license to drive steamboats, and Mr. Yowder won again. He had never seen a steamboat driver's license before and was busy reading all the fancy words on it, when the Captain looked out the window and said, "There comes the Pilot."

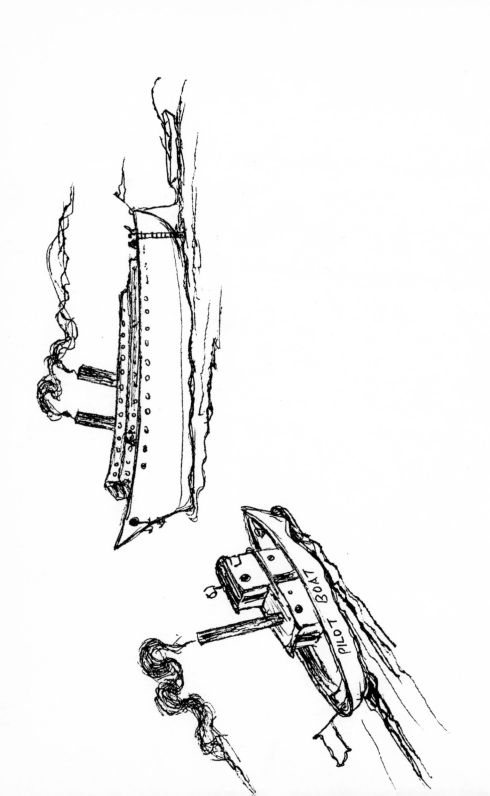

"What's a Pilot?" Mr. Yowder wanted to know, and the Captain explained to him that a Captain could drive a steamboat back and forth across the ocean, but couldn't drive it up to the bank and tie it up. The Pilot had to do that.

The Pilot had just climbed up the ladder, when the hired man hollered up the speaking tube that the engine was broken down again. He figured it would take a half hour or so to fix it, so the Captain got another chair and invited the Pilot to take a hand in their card game while they waited.

On the first hand, the Pilot bet a nickel, and Mr. Yowder bet the same. The Captain said all he had left was the steamboat, and was it all right if he bet that.

The Pilot told the Captain he couldn't bet the steamboat because he didn't own it—he just drove it for the man that did. So the Pilot and Mr. Yowder played cards, while the Captain looked out the window and drummed his fingers on the sill.

It turned out that the Pilot was no better a card player than the Captain had been. By the time the hired man called up through the speaking tube to say he had the engine running again, Mr. Yowder had won all his small change, his fancy sailor-type jackknife, his official pilot's cap and his license to drive steamboats up to the bank.

So Mr. Yowder put on his new pilot's cap, stuffed the licenses into his hip pocket and said, "Well, I reckon I'd best start this thing towards town if we're

going to get there by suppertime.'' And he walked over to the big steering wheel and picked up the speaking tube to tell the hired man to start things up.

The Captain and the Pilot raised considerable objection to his taking over the driving, but Mr. Yowder pointed out to them the rule that said it was against the law for anybody to drive a steamboat without a license—and he was the only man there that had one. It didn't seem right to them, somehow, but they had to admit that he did have the licenses, and the official caps that went with them.

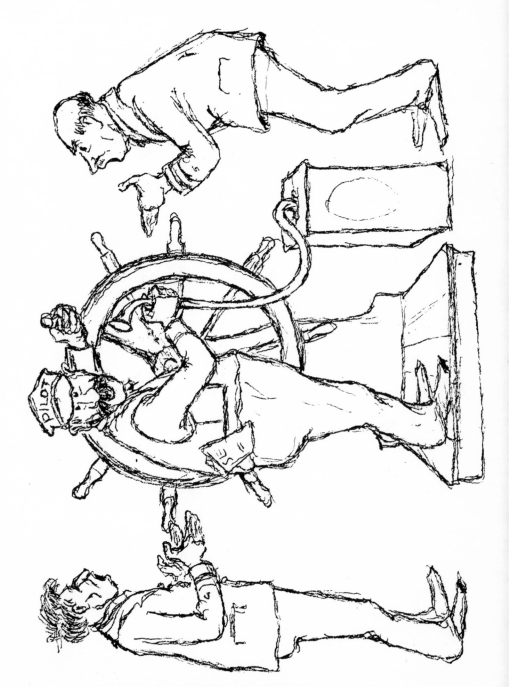

Mr. Yowder had a little trouble at first, trying to steer in a straight line, never having driven a steamboat before. But by the time he'd come in sight of town, he wasn't doing too badly. He blew the whistle a lot, and that helped him miss the boats that got in his way.

The place where he was supposed to tie the steamboat to the bank was a couple of miles up the river, at the far end of town. But Mr. Yowder could see that the river was still swarming with boats of all sizes up that way, and decided to take a shortcut.

Just before he passed the Statue of Liberty they have there, he hauled the big steering wheel clear over to the right and headed straight for the little park where Broadway Street comes down to the end of the island the town is built on.

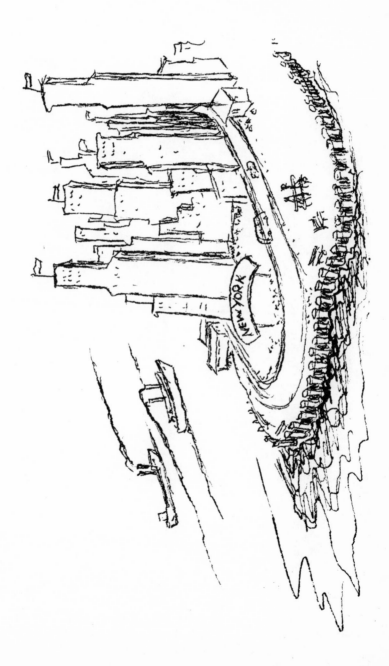

The Captain and the Pilot began to fuss and carry on about something dreadful, claiming that Mr. Yowder was going to wreck the steamboat.

Mr. Yowder told them he was doing no such thing—he was just taking a shortcut up Broadway Street. Not only would it be quicker, but he could let the passengers off right at their hotels on the way and save them taxi fares.

He also reminded them that the rule book said arguing with a steamboat Captain was called MUTINY, a very serious crime.

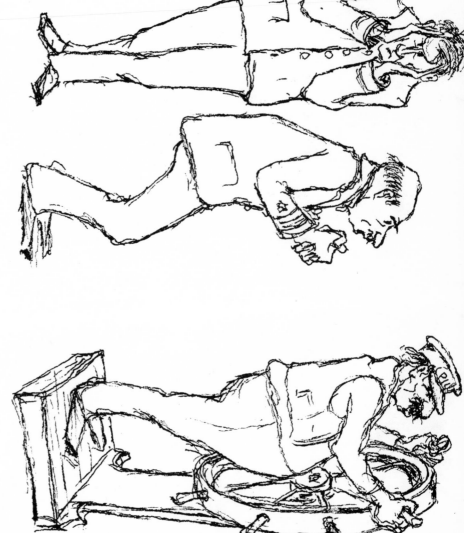

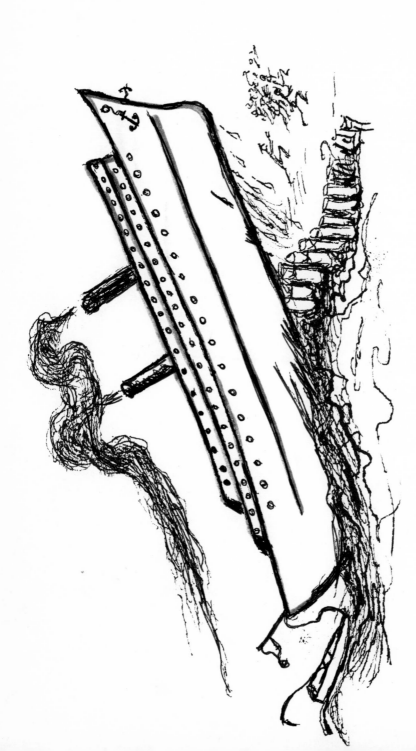

It took Mr. Yowder two tries to get the steamboat up onto the bank, but he finally made it and steered right up the middle of Broadway Street. It was a splendid sight to see, he told us later. Black smoke poured out of the steamboat's chimneys, and clouds of sparks flew from underneath where the iron bottom screeched along the cobblestones. But from the way the people in the little park and the crowds along the street carried on, you'd have thought nobody had ever driven a steamboat up Broadway before!

Policemen held up their hands and blew their whistles, dogs barked and snapped at the strange monster while automobiles, taxis and trucks tangled fenders as they ducked into alleys and side streets or drove up onto the sidewalks to get out of the steamboat's way.

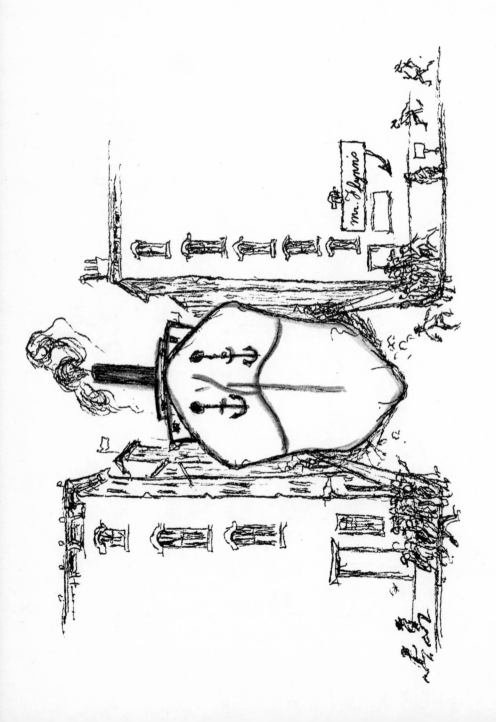

At the bend where Wall Street and Broadway come together, the high buildings are right close together, but Mr. Yowder managed to steer the steamboat between them without doing any damage except for knocking down some flagpoles that stuck out over the street, and startling a windowwasher working on a high ledge.

Once around the bend, the street was much wider, and he made better time.

But then the steamboat began to run into some of the thousands of wires that are strung like clotheslines across the streets in New York City. They are fastened to cross arms at the tops of high poles out of the way of ordinary traffic, but still too low for a steamboat to go under. Mr. Yowder hated to tear them down, but there was nothing else he could do, so he kept on driving.

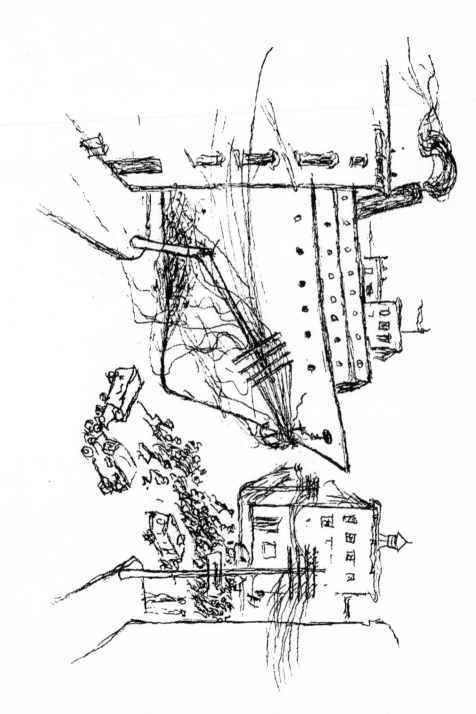

Before long there were telephone wires, electric wires and cables of all sizes hanging from the front of the steamboat and streaming behind for blocks. The fellows that owned them were running alongside waving their arms, shouting things Mr. Yowder couldn't hear. But he figured it was their fault for hanging their wires too low in the first place, so he pulled the whistle cord a time or two, in a friendly way, and drove on.

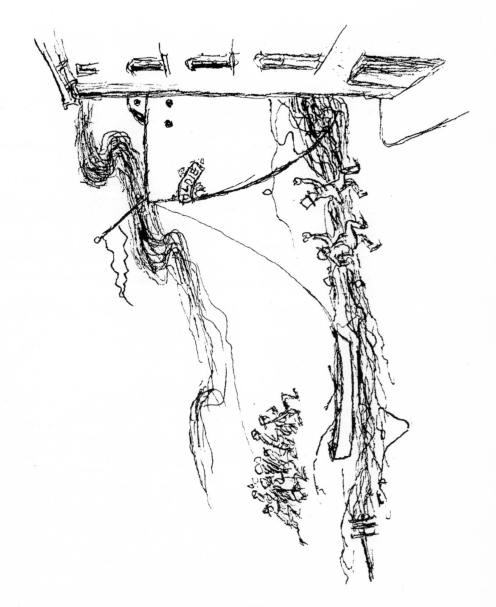

He was just about to ask the Captain which hotel he should stop at first, when he steered around an easy bend and saw an iron bridge across the street ahead. It was the first he knew of the elevated railroad that ran all over New York City, on tracks built high above the streets.

The Captain and the Pilot knew that the steamboat didn't have any brakes, so they cracked their knuckles and squinched their eyes shut while they waited for the crash. After a quick look, Mr. Yowder decided he just might be able to squeeze the steamboat under the bridge. He knew it would probably knock the boat's chimneys down, but stovepipe isn't expensive. So he called down the speaking tube for the hired man to give him full speed, blew the whistle real loud and drove straight ahead.

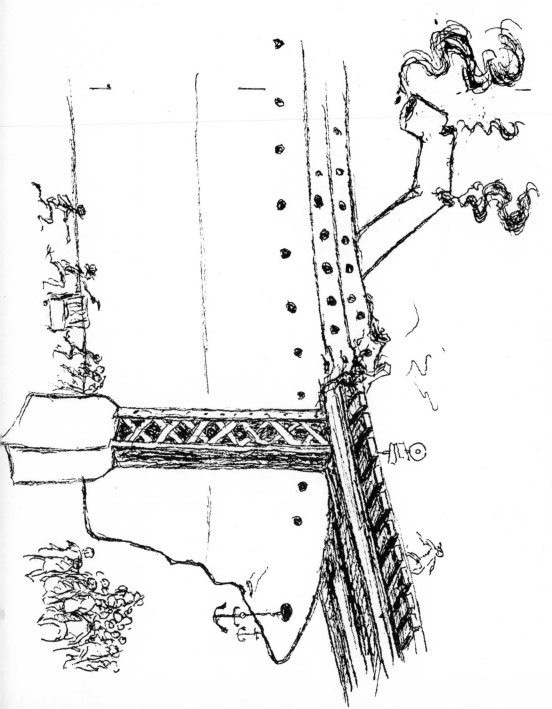

But he had misjudged the height of the steamboat by four and a half inches, they found out later. So when the screeching and squealing of bending iron was over and the dust had begun to settle, the steamboat was jammed under the bridge, tight as a cork in a bottle, completely blocking the street.

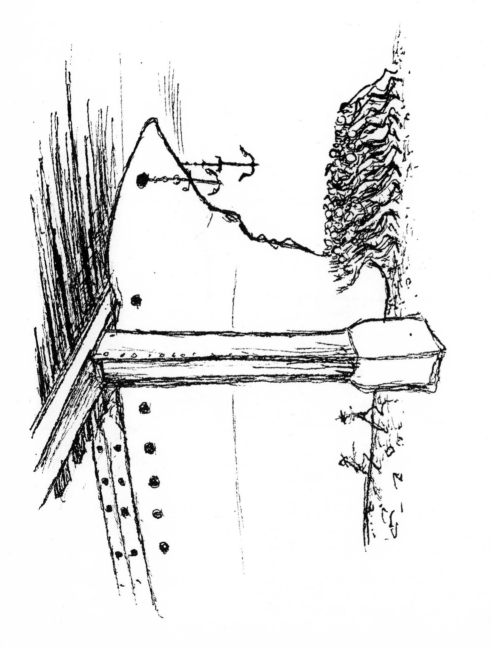

Mr. Yowder tried every way he knew to get that steamboat loose. He called down to the hired man to put the engine in reverse, while people in the street put their shoulders against the front end of the boat and pushed. But nothing worked. Even blowing the whistle didn't help.

Then he asked the Captain to hand him the Owner's Manual and Instruction Book that had come with the steamboat when it was new. It told how to get loose from mudbanks, what to do when two boats ran into each other at sea, and things like that. But nowhere was there a word about how to get out from under a railroad bridge.

Neither the Captain nor the Pilot had ever seen such an accident before, so they couldn't help him.

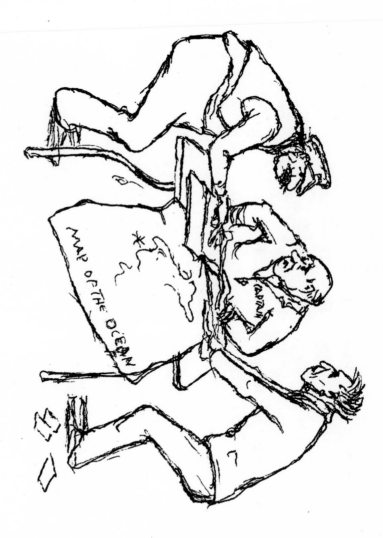

Mr. Yowder finally decided that the only thing to do was to call the hired man upstairs and have him go to the livery stable for a team of horses to pull the steamboat loose.

The hired man said he didn't know where the livery stable was, but Mr. Yowder told him just to ask a policeman. There were dozens of them down on the street waving their hands, blowing their whistles and looking in rule books.

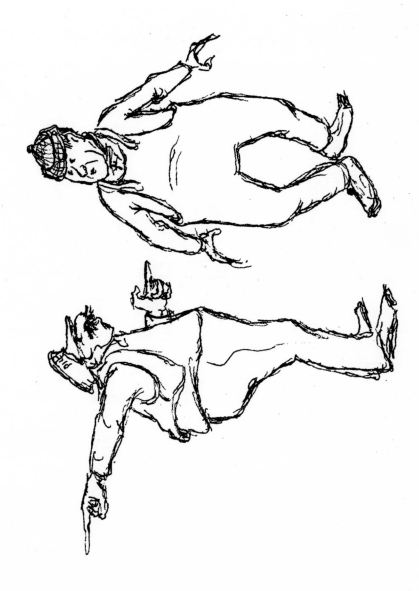

So the Captain hung the ladder over the side of the steamboat, and the hired man climbed down, asked directions from a policeman, and started off downtown to get the team of horses.

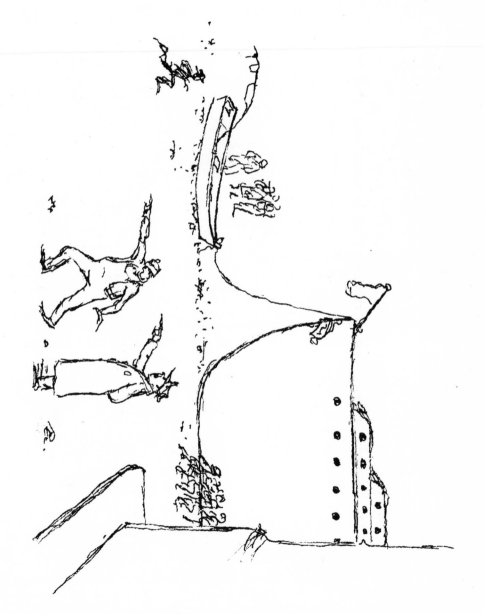

After the hired man was gone, Mr. Yowder gave the Captain and the Pilot back their official caps and their licenses, and put his battered Stetson back on. He thanked them for the ride and told them if they were ever out west of Kansas City, Missouri, to be sure to look him up.

"You're not going away leaving this boat stuck here, are you?" they wanted to know.

"It'll take an hour or two to get the horses here to pull it loose," Mr. Yowder told them. "And I'm renting this rowboat by the hour, so I have to hurry to get it back to the man I rented it from, before he closes up for the night."

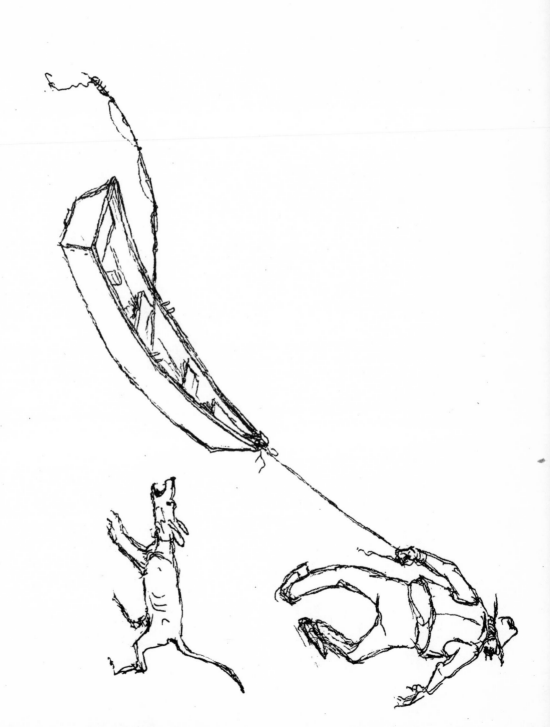

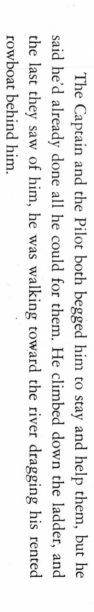

The Captain and the Pilot both begged him to stay and help them, but he said he'd already done all he could for them. He climbed down the ladder, and the last they saw of him, he was walking toward the river dragging his rented rowboat behind him.

As far as anybody knows, neither the Pilot nor the Captain ever played cards again.

GLEN ROUNDS was born in the Badlands of South Dakota and spent his boyhood on a ranch in Montana. He then prowled around the country as a sign painter, cowpuncher, mule skinner, logger, carnival barker, and lightning artist. He is a master storyteller, well known as the author-illustrator of *Ol' Paul, the Mighty Logger*, now a classic, *The Day the Circus Came to Lone Tree*, and *Mr. Yowder and the Lion Roar Capsules*. He has also written many nature books for children, among them *The Beaver: How He Works*, *Wild Orphan*, *Lone Muskrat*, and *Wildlife at Your Doorstep*.

He lives in Southern Pines, North Carolina.